SING AND READ STORYBOOK™

Ten Little Pumpkins

For my mom and dad—
thank you

ISBN 978-0-545-46862-6

12 11 10 9 8 7 6   14 15 16 17/0

Printed in the U.S.A.   40
First printing, September 2012

Book design by Jennifer Rinaldi Windau

Ten Little Pumpkins

SING AND READ STORYBOOK™

Illustrated by Jay Johnson

SCHOLASTIC INC.

Four little, five little, six little pumpkins.

Seven little, eight little, nine little pumpkins

Ten little pumpkins in a patch.

Sketching, planning, costume-making.

Decorating, sweet treats baking.

Bags of candy for the taking.

But there are pumpkins still to carve!

One little, two little, three jack-o'-lanterns.

Four little, five little, six jack-o'-lanterns.

Seven little, eight little, nine jack-o'-lanterns.

Ghostly, creepy, spooky clothing.

Shiny, sparkly,
but no peeking!

Scowls and smiles
for picture-taking!

Now it's time to trick-or-treat!

Four little, five little, six trick-or-treaters.

Seven little, eight little, nine trick-or-treaters.

Ten trick-or-treaters on Halloween night!